Alexander
the
Monkey-Sitter

Books by David Cornel DeJong

THE HAPPY BIRTHDAY UMBRELLA

THE HAPPY BIRTHDAY EGG

LOOKING FOR ALEXANDER

ALEXANDER THE MONKEY-SITTER

Alexander
the
Monkey-Sitter

by
David Cornel DeJong

Illustrated by Harvey Weiss

An Atlantic Monthly Press Book

Little, Brown and Company · Boston · Toronto

LIBRARY OF CONGRESS CATALOG CARD NO. 65-16844

Second Printing

ATLANTIC–LITTLE, BROWN BOOKS
ARE PUBLISHED BY
LITTLE, BROWN AND COMPANY
IN ASSOCIATION WITH
THE ATLANTIC MONTHLY PRESS

Published simultaneously in Canada
by Little, Brown & Company (Canada) Limited

PRINTED IN THE UNITED STATES OF AMERICA

For our own Ietje at home
and Cousin Ietje in Holland

CHAPTER ONE

YOUNG DAVID and his cat Alexander were sitting on the big white boulder in the middle of the field. They sat beneath David's large birthday umbrella, peering through each of its four windows in turn. As David twirled the umbrella slowly all its silver bells tinkled merrily.

The moment David stopped turning the umbrella, Alexander dashed after a butterfly. And as
David twirled the umbrella again, Alexander ran
back and jumped on it to box with the red blinker
tip and to peer down at David through one of the
windows.

Then Grandmother came through the gate in
the back fence looking for them. Grandmother
looked troubled. "Oh dear, I'm afraid I don't
know what this is all about, David. I had a telephone call from Mrs. Twill."

Mrs. Twill was a baby-sitter, and she was
always calling up about this and that, and very
often she was in some sort of fix. David moved
over so Grandmother could sit beside him and
Alexander.

4

"Mrs. Twill wants you to come at once and help her, David," Grandmother said. "She's out in the country."

"We could go on your bicycle, Grandmother," David said.

"But she wants you to bring your umbrella. She said: 'Tell David to bring his umbrella absolutely and positively.' She sounded so mixed up.

5

She kept jumping away from the telephone, and I heard her shout: 'Joe, Joe, you monster, get off the piano. Stop swinging on the chandelier. Don't you dare open the canary's cage.'"

"Why does she want the umbrella?" David asked.

"That I don't know, David. She did say to hurry, that the house was straight down the road and only a fifteen-minute walk. The house has a white bridge in front of it, over a creek, and she'll be watching for us."

"We'd better start," David said. "Let's go." He stood up and folded the umbrella.

"I suppose we had better, David. The poor woman really sounded as if she needed help. Mrs. Twill does seem to get herself in the worst fixes."

David was very curious about this Joe, who could swing on the chandelier and climb on the piano.

"Poor Mrs. Twill," Grandmother was saying as she climbed off the boulder. "She kept jumping away from the telephone, as if it were red hot. And all that screaming at Little Joe."

Alexander was far out in the field chasing butterflies.

CHAPTER TWO

THE BELLS on the umbrella tinkled happily as David and Grandmother hurried across the field toward the road. The sun gleamed on its red blinker top, and the wind ruffled the purple fringes which Mrs. Twill had sewed on. As they walked, Grandmother polished each of the four windows with her handkerchief.

8

Far out in the field Alexander heard the merry tinkle of the umbrella's bells and stopped chasing butterflies. It was already too late. The umbrella had reached the road, and Alexander refused to go near the road, since the time dogs chased him up the flagpole.

It took David and Grandmother just fifteen minutes to reach the white bridge across the creek. They couldn't have missed it, because there was Mrs. Twill waving her arms for them to hurry.

Then she was shouting: "I saw you come from away off. Oh, that wonderful umbrella; you can see it a mile away. But Little Joe saw it too, and what does he do? He tries to go right out of the window. And then he climbs to the top of the curtain rod, and there he hangs, upside down, watching the yellow umbrella. I don't know what to do about it."

"What a strange one Little Joe must be," Grandmother said.

"Strange isn't the word for it. You don't know half of it. I tried to pull him down, but all I got was a handful of hair and a bite on my wrist. I'll never touch him again."

Mrs. Twill showed them the teeth marks.

Grandmother could only stare at Mrs. Twill. "You must pull yourself together, Mrs. Twill," she scolded.

"Yes, yes," Mrs. Twill chattered. "But I must tell you everything first. You see, the people left this note. And the note says if Little Joe gets restless and starts screaming I am to feed him a banana. Well, I tried, but..."

Mrs. Twill had pulled the note out of her apron pocket and stood waving it under their noses. "And I'm not supposed to unlock the gate. Maybe

11

you could climb over it. But that might give him ideas, I'm sure."

"Didn't Joe's parents explain everything in their note?" Grandmother asked.

"Little Joe's parents? I doubt if they can write," Mrs. Twill babbled. "Who ever heard of such a thing?"

When David reached over to unlock the gate, she cried: "I don't think you should do that, David. Supposing he's watching? Already the little monster has opened all the faucets and flooded the bathroom. And all I have for my trouble is a handful of hair and a bite on my wrist."

Bad as Little Joe sounded, it was even more strange for a baby-sitter to go pulling hair out of his head. Usually Mrs. Twill was such a good baby-sitter, David thought to himself.

But now Mrs. Twill was actually opening the gate herself, mumbling: "What I need is a strong cup of tea, for my nerves."

"I don't understand, Mrs. Twill," Grandmother said.

"Of course you do. You must," Mrs. Twill argued. "But maybe I didn't tell you. Well, when these people called me they asked me to sit for a boy David's age, just till suppertime. Of course I said I would. But then this happens."

"You mean the little boy didn't like you?" David asked.

"How would I know, David? I hardly saw him. They decided the last minute that the boy should go along with them, but that I was to look

13

after Little Joe. And they left me this note."

Mrs. Twill waved the note at them again.

When David and Grandmother kept staring, she said: "Well, I was a little late. And they were ready to leave. And they told me just to walk in the house and take over. And I did, but when I found this monster I screamed."

"You mean Little Joe? But what is the matter with him, Mrs. Twill?" Grandmother asked.

"What is the matter with Little Joe?" Mrs. Twill screamed. "He's a monkey. A brown, wild, crazy monkey, a monster. That's why I called for you and David and his umbrella. But nobody seems to understand. I can't get him back in his cage. I don't dare."

CHAPTER THREE

"LITTLE JOE is a monkey?" David asked. It all made sense now. David could hardly wait to get into the house and meet Little Joe.

"Naturally, he's a monkey!" Mrs. Twill cried. "I wouldn't go pulling hairs out of a little boy's head, would I? I could always take care of little boys, even if they hung from curtain rods, which of course they don't. Oh, he's a monster, and he hates me."

"He's just upset because the little boy went away." Grandmother tried to comfort Mrs. Twill.

"That may be, but why didn't they tell me he could get out of his cage?"

There was no sense in answering that question. Both David and Grandmother wanted to get into the house and meet Little Joe and see what they could do.

Mrs. Twill didn't want to be left behind. She came running after them, shouting: "Oh, do be careful. He's a real monster, I tell you. Oh, and how I need a cup of tea."

As they reached the house, David saw the

16

monkey. He was hanging on two long brown arms
from the curtain rod, bobbing up and down as
David and his umbrella came closer.

It was a wonderful monkey! It was no monster at all. It had pale golden eyes and a black top-knot on its head. When they reached the front door, the monkey was right there to greet them. But Mrs. Twill backed away. "No, I just can't go near him again. I just can't!" she cried.

David opened the door and Little Joe came bouncing out and jumped into David's arms beneath the umbrella. He hugged David and chattered excitedly and didn't seem to mind Grandmother at all. All three, David and Grandmother and Little Joe, now were beneath the umbrella. Little Joe peered through each of its four windows in turn and poked at the bells to make them tinkle. He climbed to David's shoulder, chinned himself on the umbrella's spokes, and then scrambled over to the outside and reached for the blinker top.

But at that very moment Mrs. Twill screamed: "The note says he mustn't get out. Put him back inside. Quick, quick!" At the sound of her voice the monkey hurriedly scrambled beneath the

umbrella once more and then hugged David.

How could they get the open umbrella through the door? David held on to Little Joe, and Grandmother closed the umbrella just partly so that they could squeeze it through the door. The bells tinkled loudly, and the space beneath the umbrella got small and tight, but the monkey didn't mind at all. Now if only Mrs. Twill would come in so they could close the door.

Mrs. Twill didn't come in. All she did was to shout: "Shut the door. Oh, shut the door. I'll run around the house and through the back door and I'll make a cup of tea. My nerves are gone, gone, gone..." She banged the door shut, and they heard her running away.

Grandmother said: "David, I think I'd better look after Mrs. Twill. Now you and Little Joe are doing fine. He likes you."

Grandmother hurried through the house to the kitchen to meet Mrs. Twill. Little Joe was so happy beneath the umbrella and seemed to like David so much that he kept hugging the umbrella stem and David in turn. He didn't even mind when David closed the umbrella. He played with the bells and fringe.

Now David could see what damage the monkey had done. Magazines were torn up, books lay everywhere, water dripped from fallen vases, the curtains had been dragged to the floor, rugs were all in a heap, and the chandelier was tilting crazily. But as David looked at all the mess, Little Joe came trotting happily along and even helped him straighten out things.

But then Mrs. Twill screamed through a crack in the kitchen door: "Do be careful, David. He's a real monster. Do put him back in his cage and lock him up. And come and have a cup of tea with us." Then Little Joe tore away and dashed up the drapes at the other end of the room, hand over foot, chattering and chittering wildly.

Mrs. Twill banged the door shut. David coaxed

the monkey down. "It's all right, Little Joe. She can't hurt you," he crooned. Little Joe came down again, still shivering, and hid his face in David's hair. It was plain that Little Joe was just as afraid of Mrs. Twill as she was of him.

David stroked the poor monkey's head. "Now, Little Joe, just show me where your cage is," he whispered.

Little Joe did nothing of the kind. Over David's shoulder he peered anxiously at the kitchen door.

He had better find Little Joe's cage, David thought. Once he had, he might be able to coax the monkey inside with a banana.

CHAPTER FOUR

WHERE TO LOOK for the monkey's cage in a strange house?

When David started looking, Little Joe followed him, chattering and clinging close. Only when they came near the kitchen door was he frightened. He was afraid of Mrs. Twill's voice coming from behind it.

Then David came to one other place where the monkey wouldn't follow him. On the other side of a room which had to belong to a boy, David saw the door standing ajar. But as soon as David walked toward it, Little Joe made angry crying sounds and threw things all over the boy's room. There was nothing to do but lead the monkey back to the living room and the umbrella.

"I tell you what we'll do, Little Joe," David said. "I'll open the umbrella and you can sit and play under it. I'll go and find your cage. It can't be all that bad."

David opened the umbrella wide, and at the sight of it Little Joe's eyes became as round as little golden moons. When the umbrella was wide open, he got beneath it and made faces through the windows. The next moment he got very curious about the handle of the umbrella with its long curved neck and flamingo head. He sat down and jibbered at it.

Now to find the cage and a banana. Once more David hurried across the boy's room. This time he saw that behind the half-open door there was a large and handsome monkey cage. It had swings

28

and even a small table and chair, not to mention a little painted bed. But there was also something which didn't belong there. A broom. And on the end of the broom rested a whole banana. The door of the cage was standing wide open.

David stared. He could imagine what must have happened. Mrs. Twill must have come armed with a broom, possibly screaming at the top of her voice and pushing the banana with the broom through the cage door. And Little Joe, terrified at the broom and Mrs. Twill's screaming, must have come leaping right out. Without looking back, Mrs. Twill must have run to the kitchen and locked herself in.

Now what to do? Little Joe must be terribly frightened of the broom. He'd have to take the

30

broom out first, and then...He was still trying to figure out what to do next when Mrs. Twill called from the kitchen: "David, where are you? Do come and have your tea."

At the sound of Mrs. Twill's voice Little Joe jumped. Before David could get to him he had lowered the umbrella. With it flapping over him like a tall yellow cone, and the brown monkey

feet paddling underneath, Little Joe went scampering toward the front door. He pushed a long arm from under the umbrella and reached for the latch.

He was fast and nimble. When David reached the door, the monkey had already jumped through and onto the porch railing. The umbrella had caught and pulled open. Little Joe sailed away beneath the umbrella, using it as a parachute. With the help of a stiff breeze he flew across the lawn toward the bridge.

This time it was David who screamed for help.

CHAPTER FIVE

BENEATH the big umbrella Little Joe went running down the road. The little gate on the bridge hadn't stopped him for a moment. He sailed clear across it. David ran after him, and after him came Grandmother. Mrs. Twill came running behind her, again screaming at the top of

her voice. Each time she screamed, Little Joe
leaped up in the air and sailed higher and faster
beneath the umbrella.

Grandmother stopped Mrs. Twill to tell her
to stop her screaming. It seemed to work, because
Little Joe looked as if he were coming to a stop.
When David called: "Little Joe, wait for me," the
monkey actually stopped and peered back at him
through one of the umbrella's windows. But he
must have seen Mrs. Twill, who was now trying
so hard not to scream that she stood in the middle
of the road wringing her hands.

The very sight of her started Little Joe going again. Straight down the road he went, straight for town. No matter how fast David ran, he couldn't catch up.

Straight into town Little Joe bobbed with all the umbrella's bells jangling madly. Up in the air he rose and down he came again, with his brown feet pattering down the middle of the pavement.

Little Joe reached the main street of town and kept going past the flagpole behind David's house. David came pounding after him, but Grandmother was still trying to calm Mrs. Twill. People came running out of their houses, and Mrs. Twill shouted at everyone she saw: "There's a monster loose. Catch that monster."

Mr. Bim ran out of his tailor shop. He saw

David's famous umbrella go bouncing by with a pair of hairy legs beneath it and David running behind it. "Oh no, there's something wrong with my eyes. I'm seeing things," Mr. Bim shouted, and hopped back into his shop. He came out again with a large laundry bag and ran after David and the umbrella.

Sam popped out of his second-hand shop. He gaped and gasped, and then he grabbed a butterfly net and joined the chase, somewhere between Grandmother and Mrs. Twill.

Past Jack and Joe's Filling Station and Greasing Palace raced the umbrella with the furry feet beneath it. Both Jack and Joe piled into their jeep and followed, almost running over Mr. Bim.

With all that crowd behind him, Little Joe suddenly dashed off the road and into the field with the big white boulder in it. Only David followed him now.

Jack and Joe stopped their jeep and picked up Mr. Bim and Sam. They couldn't cross the field,

so they kept going down the road to circle the block. Grandmother had pulled Mrs. Twill onto the curb. She sat there, too tired now to open her mouth.

David galloped across the field, but by the time he reached the big boulder the monkey was already more than halfway across the field.

Nothing could stop Little Joe. Nothing.

But then something did!

CHAPTER SIX

Poor ALEXANDER!

When he saw David and Grandmother leave the field and go down the road beneath the big umbrella, he meowed. But he did not dare to follow them.

He no longer felt like chasing butterflies.

Slowly he walked back to the house, where he climbed to the top of the grape arbor. From there he saw the yellow umbrella disappear down the road.

Alexander closed his eyes. He fell asleep. He woke up again and again, and each time he looked for the umbrella to come back. He slept again. But then he woke up with a start.

He heard the wild jangling of the umbrella's silver bells. He saw the umbrella come skipping and jumping across the field, past the large white boulder. Only David could be beneath it, because it came so fast. It went bouncing up and down wildly. David must be playing a game.

Wide awake now, Alexander crouched and waited, his tail whipping with excitement.

The umbrella was coming by leaps and bounds. Alexander got ready to pounce. He was going to surprise David.

When the umbrella was directly beneath him, Alexander jumped. He landed, wobbled and dug in with his claws. The umbrella leaped high and went zigzagging every which way, and then kept rocking and jerking so much it almost made him dizzy. David certainly was acting frisky. Holding on with his claws, Alexander tried to get a look at David through one of the windows.

When he pushed his face down against the window, the umbrella went wild. It went so wild that Alexander couldn't even get a glimpse of David. The umbrella hopped high up in the air and landed right on top of the empty trash barrel.

44

And now the umbrella sat over the barrel like a
roof. In the dark barrel Alexander couldn't see
David at all, but David surely was making a weird
racket in there.

At the same time Alexander heard the pounding of feet across the field and through the back gate. And there came David—David, who was supposed to be in the barrel beneath the umbrella, and David was shouting: "Good for you, Alexander. You did it. You caught him."

Now, too, he heard a lot of shouting at the front of the house. And Alexander saw, piling out of a jeep, Jack and Joe, and Mr. Bim with a large laundry bag, and Sam with a butterfly net. It was just too much. Alexander jumped from the top of the umbrella and into the pear tree.

What he saw from the pear tree didn't make him feel any better. Joe lifted the umbrella from the barrel, Jack tipped the barrel, Sam slapped the butterfly net over its mouth, and Mr. Bim

stood holding the large laundry bag wide open.

Alexander climbed higher. From there he saw
Grandmother across the field, holding on to Mrs.
Twill.

47

Alexander looked toward the barrel again. Now he saw a wild animal, all fur and legs and teeth, thrashing around in Sam's butterfly net. Then everybody pushed the creature into a laundry bag.

Alexander ran. He climbed to the highest limb of the tree and pretended to be looking at a little hard, green pear. It was better to keep an eye on it than on all the madness underneath.

He didn't even look down when David cried: "Oh, let me have him. Just let me hold Little Joe. He's afraid." But out of the corner of his eye Alexander saw the men hurrying to the jeep with the bouncing, wriggling thing still in the laundry bag.

Alexander closed his eyes. He heard David run across the field to join Grandmother and Mrs. Twill. A little later David and Grandmother came back together, calling: "Alexander, Alexander, where are you?" Alexander pretended to be hearing and seeing nothing at all.

Then David and Grandmother also went to the jeep. "Mrs. Twill says she's too tired and upset to take another step. She's going home for a cup of tea, and we're not to wait for her," he heard Grandmother explain. When Alexander took just one little look, he saw that David was already in the jeep and was lifting the horrible creature out of the laundry bag. He saw the ugly beast put his long arms around David's neck and hug him.

It was awful. He couldn't stand to look at it. He stared very hard at the little green pear only. He heard, but he did not see, the jeep drive away with everybody in it, including that wild beast which had been beneath David's umbrella.

CHAPTER SEVEN

THE JEEP was ready to go, but then David remembered his umbrella. He ran back to pick it up. They might be needing it for Little Joe.

Then they were on their way, with Joe driving and Little Joe clinging for dear life to David, hugging him hard and keeping his eyes shut

52

until they were a good way down the road.

What had become of poor Alexander, David wondered. Alexander, who had been the real hero and now was missing all the fun. He heard Grandmother tell the men what had happened and why Mrs. Twill was in such a state. Still, it must have been Mrs. Twill who had driven Little Joe wild by poking the cage door open with a broom and then screaming and running away, leaving the broom and the banana behind and the cage door wide open. David hadn't had a chance yet to tell Grandmother about the broom. And he wasn't even going to mention the broom as long as Little Joe kept clinging to him for protection.

But long before they reached the house, Little Joe was himself again. He was particularly inter-

ested in Mr. Bim's little black beard and tugged at it to see if it would come off. Mr. Bim didn't mind. It was a very cheerful ride back to the house.

The gate on the bridge was standing wide open, just as Mrs. Twill had left it. David decided he'd carry Little Joe across the bridge and close the gate. After all, Mrs. Twill's note had said it should be closed. But Little Joe refused to leave the jeep until David had opened his umbrella. Then he hopped to David's shoulder. From the bridge they watched Grandmother thanking everybody who had helped. Jack and Joe and Mr. Bim and Sam all had to hurry back to their shops, which they had left wide open in the middle of the day.

As the jeep drove away, David twirled the umbrella to keep Little Joe happy. Neither he nor Grandmother had told each other that they would go and sit with Little Joe till his people came back. But he knew they would. And when Grandmother came hurrying across the bridge and cried: "Why, David, now you and I will monkey-sit. And I think it will be more fun than a picnic—more fun than a barrel of monkeys," he knew exactly what she meant.

56

Still he said: "Except, Grandmother."

"Except what, David?"

"Except it would have been even more wonderful if Alexander had come along. After all, look what Alexander did."

"Now, David," Grandmother laughed, "Alexander is much happier at home. He's had enough monkey business to last him a lifetime. Besides, Little Joe'd be so scared he wouldn't be doing what he's doing now."

Because Little Joe had climbed to the top of the umbrella and stood clinging to its red blinker top, like a sailor to the top of a mast, watching the jeep disappear down the road.

5/2/4 DeJong, David Cornel

Alexander the monkey-sitter

 32227

DATE DUE

MY 25 72			
OC 25 72			
NY 12 73			
DE 21 73			
SE 3 74			
MY 16 75